An Mei's
Strange and Wondrous Journey

by Stephan Molnar-Fenton

Illustrated by Vivienne Flesher

A DK Ink Book
DK PUBLISHING, INC.

A Melanie Kroupa Book

Ink

DK Publishing, Inc.
95 Madison Avenue
New York, New York 10016

Visit us on the World Wide Web at
http://www.dk.com

Library of Congress Cataloging-in-Publication Data

Molnar-Fenton, Stephan.
    An-Mei's strange and wondrous jour-
ney / by Stephan Molnar-Fenton ;
illustrated by Vivienne Flesher. —1st ed.
        p.   cm.
    "A Melanie Kroupa book."
    Summary: Six-year-old An Mei tells
the story of how she was born in China
and came to live in America.
    ISBN 0-7894-2477-0
    [1. Chinese Americans—Fiction. 2.
Emigration and immigration—Fiction.]
I. Flesher, Vivienne, ill.   II. Title.
PZ7.F3425An   1998   97-31001
[E]—dc21   CIP
                                  AC

Book design by Chris Hammill Paul.
The text of this book is set in
15 point Diotima.

Printed and bound in the
United States of America

First Edition, 1998

2 4 6 8 10 9 7 5 3

For my wife, Dorothy; my
children, Gabriel, Sarton,
and Anjelica-Tao An Mei;
and all the beautiful people
of China. Thank you.
          S. M.-F.

For Ward Schumaker.
          V. F.

安美

My name is An Mei. It is Chinese
for "beautiful peace."
    I was born on a train as it passed
through a long, dark tunnel.

When the train broke into the light, I saw my mother's face for the first time. Her black eyes sparkled brighter than the sun. And on her blouse was a white swan swimming on a blue lake.

When the train stopped, my mother tucked me inside her coat and we got off. The air was cool and shimmered where it touched the wheels of the train.

We walked down a wide dirt road that twisted and turned as though it couldn't make up its mind which way to go.

Men and women carried straw baskets filled with oranges, chestnuts, mushrooms, eels, and balls of fried rice. A woman was serving a bowl of steaming hot noodles to an old man wearing a big yellow hat.

Cages with small birds were balanced on a rock wall. Little children watched us as we walked by. They were sucking on sticks of sugarcane and roasting sweet potatoes over an upside-down metal can. The flames flickered and snapped like a dragon's tongue.

Without warning, the road
ended. A large bird with round
golden eyes circled above us. It
hooted twice and flew away.

My mother took a small brush
from her pocket and painted a
red dot on my forehead. The
soft bristles of the brush tickled.
Then my mother wrapped me
in a warm quilted blanket and
placed me on the stone steps of
the Wuhan orphanage.

I felt her hand touch my
cheek before she disappeared.
As she walked away, I could
hear the wind whip against the
metal buttons of her long coat.

I was alone. I closed my eyes
and fell asleep.

When I woke up, a woman wearing white was holding me. Her merry eyes danced as she whispered my name. Then she gently placed me in a crib and tucked the four corners of my blanket around me.

The little girl lying beside me was fast asleep, her breathing as regular as the ticktock of a clock.

In the large room there were many cribs, and all the babies were asleep. I listened, but not one moved or made a peep. Then I heard the same sound the wind had made as my mother walked away.

I looked. But it was only the leaves of a bamboo tree brushing against the windowpane.

The days passed. Then weeks and months. Ice drew pictures on the windowpanes, and snow wrapped a blanket around the branches of the bamboo tree.

One day a man with a bushy black beard and skin the color of an oyster shell appeared. He leaned his arms on the rail of my crib and watched me.

Then he picked me up. He held me as if he was afraid I would break, and he smelled of places I had never been. His words were foreign and had no shape.

He rocked me back and forth, back and forth, in his strong arms, and I felt like a small boat on a wide river. I opened my eyes and the man smiled. His black beard fluttered like a crow's feathers. Soon his words became a song. I stopped crying and listened.

Then he wrapped me snugly in my quilted blanket and carried me away. I heard a scary sound and felt the plane rise into the air, but the man held me tight and sang to me again.

We crossed water so wide and blue I thought it would never end. Day became night. And as the man fed me milk that was warm and sweet, I watched his face. I never blinked—not even once.

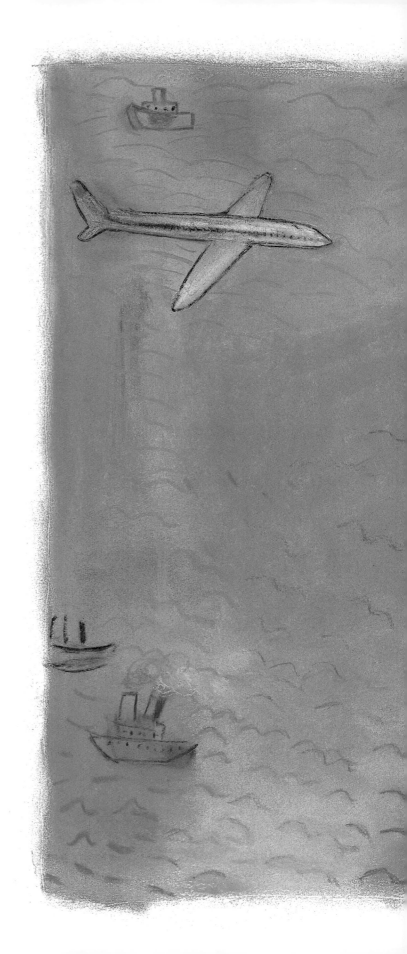

At the end of our journey, a woman with eyes as round and gray as pearls waited for us. She gave us both a great big hug and laughed and cried at the same time. I turned away and watched her from the corner of my eye.

Then they drove me to my new home. The sky was low and dark, and the moon was rising fast. They placed me in a red wooden crib. In the corner sat a soft panda bear. When I squeezed the panda's tummy, music filled the room. Everything looked bright and scary and new.

The man turned on a small yellow light, and the woman folded my blanket over me. I tried to keep my eyes open, but I soon fell asleep.

The days passed. Then weeks and months. I grew and grew and soon learned the names of the things that had once seemed strange and new.

Every morning when I woke, the woman with the gray eyes would hold me and we would sit on the front steps. Flowers as bright as fireworks dotted the trees. Children on their way to school ran by and shouted my name—"Hello, An Mei!"

Every night the man with the black beard would take me for a walk by the river. An old owl perched high in an oak tree made a noise that sounded like Chinese. I wondered if he remembered me. The man named the noisy owl His Royal Emperor.

Then one summer day the woman took me to the park. She lifted me high and placed me on a swing. She smiled, but I turned away.

The swing began to sway. I could see the sky slip and the ground rise. The wind rushed over me. I was falling!

But before I fell all the way, the woman reached out and caught me.

I looked up into her round gray eyes and called her Mommy. Her eyes sparkled brighter than the sun.

On my sixth birthday, my daddy dug a deep, round hole and planted twin bamboo trees. My mother and I stamped down the cool, dark earth with our bare feet. A worm crawled between my toes. And as the sun began to set, we filled the hole with water.

That night a sound woke me
up. I jumped out of bed and
stood very still. My room was
dark except for the puddle of
moonlight that spilled across
the floor.

I heard the sound the wind
had made against the buttons
of my mother's coat when
she left me on the steps.
I called out.

Daddy came in, listened, and pointed. It was only the leaves of the bamboo tree brushing against my windowpane. I climbed into my bed. Daddy turned on the lamp. His black beard was so freckled with white, I whispered that he looked like a panda bear.

When he thought I was asleep, he kissed my forehead, tucked my blanket around me, and turned off the light. Then he tiptoed out. I knew I was safe.

That night I had a dream about a train passing through a long, dark tunnel. At the end of the tunnel was a white swan swimming on a blue lake. It was here that my strange and wondrous journey had begun.

One year to the day after I first met my daughter, An Mei, I began writing this book. This is her story and, in many ways, the story of thousands of other babies from every country in the world who have made the strange and wondrous journey to an adoptive family.

Why do parents put their children up for adoption? There are hundreds of reasons—perhaps as many reasons as there are families. It is not because parents don't love their children; this is usually one of the hardest decisions parents ever make. Sometimes parents realize they are too young, have too many other children, or do not have enough money to care for the baby. Usually their reasons involve wanting a better life for their child than they could provide.

There are special circumstances in China that lead many parents to place their children up for adoption. China has more than one and a half billion people—five times as many as the United States—and if this number keeps growing, soon there may not be enough food or jobs or homes for everyone. In the early 1980s the Chinese government enacted a new law that allows families to have only one child. Many families who find themselves expecting a second child feel they have no choice but to allow that child to be adopted. As conditions in China improve, however, this policy will soften, allowing families greater freedom of choice.

In addition, in China the firstborn son has a special position in the family: He inherits the family property, cares for the parents when they are old, and carries on the family name. This tradition is many centuries old and is only slowly giving way to the idea that daughters are just as special as sons. Some parents, for whom this tradition is still strong, decide to put their first child up for adoption if she is a girl, so that they can try again for a son.

An old Chinese legend says that the dragon takes a thousand shapes and changes color in order to protect its people. Like the dragon, love takes many forms. The red dot on An Mei's forehead is a traditional symbol of love—and it was her mother's prayer that An Mei's journey would lead her to a life of beauty and joy.

Stephan Molvray Fenton